Gaby and Her Big Surprise

Written by Tammy Crawford

Illustrated by Misty Morgan

AuthorHouse™
1663 Liberty Drive
Bloomington, IN 47403
www.authorhouse.com
Phone: 833-262-8899

ISBN: 978-1-4389-3323-8 (sc)

Print information available on the last page.

Published by AuthorHouse 11/16/2022

authorHOUSE®

To all of my grandchildren,
Mickale, Gaby, Dristen, and Ambria.

"Hurray, Hurray! Yep, yep, hurray! It is going to be a wonderful day. Today is my birthday!" Gaby excitedly hurried through her chores so she could go outside to play with her new puppy!

"Come on, Freckles; we will go and find my other furry friends. Maybe we can share a tea party down by the lake." Gaby happily skipped off toward the forest path in search of her little forest friends.

As she skipped through the forest, she did not see any of her friends around. *I wonder where everyone could be?* she thought. Her friends were always there to welcome her to come and play. Did they forget she was coming by today?

Oh, yeah! I see Henrietta, a very busy furry white rabbit. "Hello Henrietta, how are you this sunny summer day? Freckles and I are going to have tea down by the lake. Would you like to come with us?"

"I am so sorry, Gaby, but I am afraid I can't. I need to run over to see Mr. Cleaver. He is not feeling well today. An ornery old beaver is just what he is."

"I do hope he feels better soon. Maybe I could bring by some of mama's chicken soup a little while later."

Walking a little slower, Gaby continued down the forest path. *Could that be Chippers? It is Chippers.* "Hello, Chippers, you silly squirrel; you seem in such a hurry. You almost ran us over! Freckles and I are going to have tea down by the lake. Please, will you come?"

"Oh, Gaby, I really wish I could, but Mama is sending me to do an errand, and then Mama said I must get my fluffy tail right back home!"

"Oh, Chippers, that's all right. Everyone seems to be a little busy today. Maybe when your errand is finished your mother will send you out to play."

All Gaby wanted was to share her birthday with her friends, but it seems no one had any time to spare. "Well, Freckles, it looks like it's just you and me."

"I guess we will just go back home." Turning around, Gaby found Billy, a little bear cub, standing in the forest path. "Hi, Billy," Gaby said a little sadly. "I suppose you must be very busy and need to be on your way. It seems that is all I have heard from everyone today."

"Then you will be happy to know that I was out looking for you, Gaby," Billy said.

"You were out looking for me? You're not too busy today?" Gaby asked excitedly.

"I wanted to wish you a happy birthday! Would you like to go down by the lake and share some tea, Gaby?"

"Oh, Billy, that sounds like so much fun."

While chatting along the path, Gaby told Billy why all their friends were busy. Then, as they were reaching the lake, Gaby looked up and had a surprise of all surprises. All her friends were there! Henrietta was there, Mr. Cleaver was there, and even Chippers the silly old squirrel was there.

26

"Surprise! Happy birthday, Gaby!" They all yelled to her.

Gaby was completely surprised. All her friends were giving her a surprise birthday party with tea, and a birthday cake too!

For the rest of the afternoon, Gaby and her friends played, drank all the tea, and ate birthday cake until they were so full they thought their tummies would burst!

Gaby gave each of her friends a great big hug. The time to go home came much too fast. Gaby and Freckles had to go.

"See you all tomorrow!" They heard her yell.

The End

Printed in the United States
by Baker & Taylor Publisher Services